# FLYIN FURBALLS

# *Downfall*

## DONOVAN BIXLEY

upstart press

Dedicated to the winners of my
Totally Pawsome character design competition.
Congratulations to: Mindi Bosher with The Mighty Osman,
and Amelia Ferguson with Furgus McLongtail.
You'll find their creations somewhere in this book!
Also look out for the runners-up:
Wing Commander Giggles by Luke Dickinson,
Baron Cosmo McArelsin by Magnus Fraser,
and Snowy von Fluffytail by Yaran Hao.

A catalogue record for this book is available from the
National Library of New Zealand

ISBN 978-1-988516-61-5

An Upstart Press Book
Published in 2020 by Upstart Press Ltd
Level 6, BDO Tower, 19-21 Como St, Takapuna
Auckland 0622, New Zealand

Printed by 1010 Printing International Limited, China

# MEET SOME OF THE CHARACTERS AT CATs HQ

**Claude D'Bonair** learnt to fly from his father, who was a stunt pilot and adventurer. Claude is the youngest pilot ever to be accepted into the CATs Air Corps. He's also the only cat to be awarded the CATs Cross, the Purple Paw *and* the Double Cross.

**Syd Fishus** flew the first airplanes with Claude's father before the war. He has many bad habits, but he's a fearless dogfighter and Claude's most loyal friend.

**Major Ginger Tom** thinks he's the cat's pyjamas. He is heir to the Earl of Cheshire and his family descends from Queen Ginger the First. He lets nothing get in the way of his ambitious dreams … and schemes.

**Manx** is HQ's brilliant mechanic. She secretly worked alongside the famous aircraft designer Catproni, helping build his new fighter planes. CATs' head engineer also has her paws full looking after her two sisters: fidgeting **Wigglebum**, and ever-curious **Picklepurr**.

**Mr Tiddles** is the General's scretary. He loves to sing and was on stage in the musical of Major Tom's autobiography. He also likes model-making.

**Commander Katerina Snookums** is the head of CATs Air Corps. She's a great judge of character. **General Fluffington** is her right-paw cat. He has trouble accepting that not all dogs are bad DOGZ.

**Mrs Cushion** pretends to be the General's tea lady, but she's really keeping an eye on CATs' secret operations.

**C-for** is HQ's resident scientist, forever dreaming up crazy new gadgets — which always seem to work in unexpected ways.

# MEET SOME OF THE WHITE PAW REBELS

**Rex** is the leader of The White Paw rebels, with a mission to defeat the DOGZ and restore the true dog king to the throne. Rex was trained in politics, history and painting. He uses his artistic skills to make funny newspaper cartoons mocking the DOGZ.

**Buster** is Rex's second-in-command. He was an officer in the DOGZ army but he has always stayed loyal to the true dog king, making him a valuable double agent for The White Paw.

**Baron von Wolfred** was once the most feared pilot in the DOGZ air force (where he was known as The Red Setter). After making friends with Claude, he has joined forces with The White Paw.

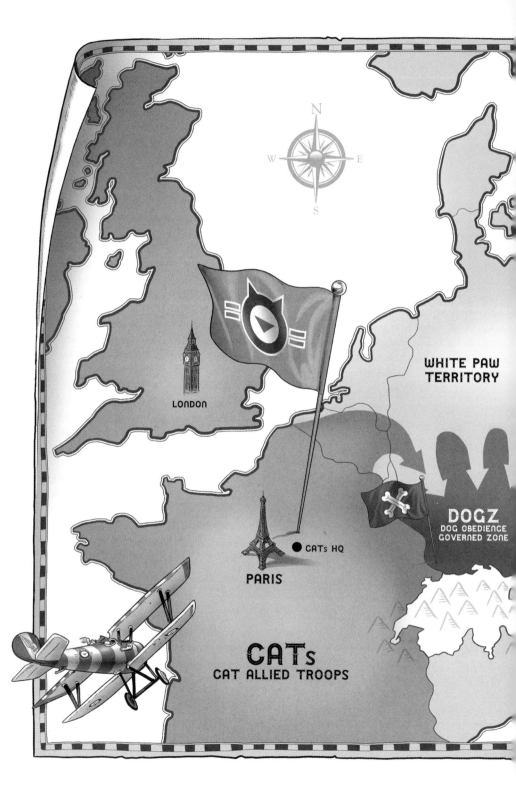

BERLIN

WHITE PAW
TERRITORY

# EUROPE 1918

Cats and dogs once lived together in peace. That was before a pack calling themselves DOGZ took over the kingdoms of Central Europe. Now, after years of war, the Cat Allied Troops (CATs) have forced the DOGZ back into their mountain stronghold. Only with the help of their secret allies, The White Paw, can CATs save Europe from going to the DOGZ.

# CHATEAU FUR-DE-LYS

CATs headquarters (HQ) on the outskirts of Paris.
Secret passageways in the chateau lead to the
underground catacombs beneath Paris.

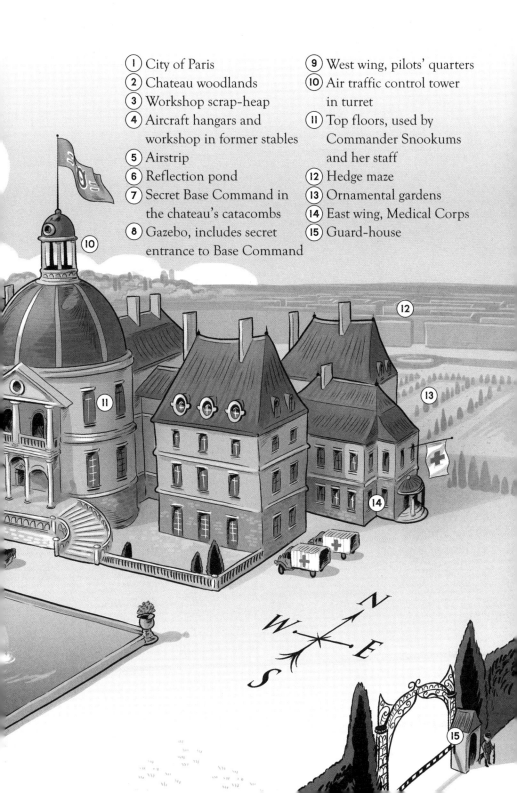

1. City of Paris
2. Chateau woodlands
3. Workshop scrap-heap
4. Aircraft hangars and workshop in former stables
5. Airstrip
6. Reflection pond
7. Secret Base Command in the chateau's catacombs
8. Gazebo, includes secret entrance to Base Command
9. West wing, pilots' quarters
10. Air traffic control tower in turret
11. Top floors, used by Commander Snookums and her staff
12. Hedge maze
13. Ornamental gardens
14. East wing, Medical Corps
15. Guard-house

# CHAPTER 1

'Tug my tail and tell me it's time for tuna,' said Major Ginger Tom. The most famous dogfighter at Cat Allied Troops, or CATs as they were known, was on a mission deep within enemy DOGZ territory.

Major Tom flew his plane up a wooded valley, directly towards the DOGZ stronghold of Hundestein Castle. Dozens of anti-aircraft guns and Howlitzer cannons were aimed at him, yet Major Tom was totally fearless. This was *not* because Major Tom was a courageous daredevil, but because he was flying a secret mission … as a spy for the DOGZ army!

Major Tom circled above the castle. From here he could see clearly into the courtyard. It was packed with DOGZ soldiers and military equipment. One of the DOGZ soldiers was using flags to signal to Major Tom.

*Excellent*, thought Major Tom.
Everything was prepared for his plan.

Katdom's most famous pussycat
had been plotting against his own
kind all along. Major Tom gave
an evil smirk and sped off in the
direction of CATs HQ, near Paris.
He was returning for a surprise
demonstration, where he would show off the latest
technology installed in his plane. *They'll get a big
surprise alright*, Major Tom chuckled to himself. But
first he'd make it look as if he'd been caught up in
a daring dogfight. That was easy. Everyone always
believed his crazy stories ... and Major Tom was well
practised at inventing heroic things he hadn't done.

Now that his plans were about to be fulfilled,
Major Tom needed to take extra care not to be
discovered as a spy by his fellow CATs. He was
particularly keen to be rid of Claude D'Bonair.
That upstart pilot had managed to foil Major Tom's
schemes again and again. It was time for Claude's
nine lives to run out, once and for all.

Claude D'Bonair edged forward on stealthy cat paws. The young pilot was entering the hedge maze behind the grand chateau, which served as CATs HQ. The maze was a risky spot — it was a perfect place to be ambushed, and somewhere in the leafy labyrinth lurked two attackers. Claude would need to use all his skill in the martial art of Meow-zaki if he was going to defeat his assailants.

As Claude came to a turn in the maze, he saw a flicker of movement from the corner of his eye. He twisted around — just in time to see a furious blur of fuzz flying at him. It was shouting the unmistakable cry of …

# MEOW-THA KI!

With practised skill, Claude moved into
Coiling Snake pose, but then a shadow fell
across his back. Instantly, he knew it was a trap.
Claude spun around as the second attacker
came swooping towards him in the Meow-zaki
position of Pouncing Tiger.

However, Claude was expertly trained.

In the flutter of a heartbeat, he twirled sideways.

The two attackers sailed past him, without
disturbing a single whisker on his face.

They collided mid-air and crashed to the ground with a thud — while Claude stood in the peaceful stance known as Laughing Crane, with a smug grin on his face.

But when his two attackers didn't move, Claude dropped the pose and rushed to where they had fallen.

'Wigglebum? Picklepurr?'

He'd been teaching the two kittens Meow-zaki, the ancient martial art Claude had learned from his father. What would their big sister, Manx, think when she learnt they had been knocked out?

Claude crouched over the poor wee kits — and that's when they flung themselves upon him. Their little paws dug into Claude's weakest spots and he rolled backwards with his two attackers pinning him down.

飛び鳳凰

Crouching
Cobra

巻かをへび
はするコブラ

Flying Phoenix

Coiling Snake

'What kind of move do you call that?' came a voice from behind them. CATs' head engineer, Manx, stood with her paws on her hips and a quizzical expression on her face.

'Playing dead,' said Picklepurr.

'An' this oneth called Tickle Torture,' laughed Wigglebum with her distinctive lisp. She leapt up and down on Claude, tickling him mercilessly.

**Laughing Crane**

**Stinging Scorpion**

**Pouncing Tiger**

'Surrender, Claude, or die laughing!' commanded Picklepurr.

Wigglebum looked at her big sister. 'We're being gwate heroeth,' she explained.

'Great heroes?' questioned Manx. 'Like Claude?'

'Noooo!' said Pickle. 'Like Major Tom.'

'*I'm* Major Tom,' cried Wiggle.

'No! *I* was Major Tom long before you were!' wailed Pickle. The two kittens forgot all about Claude and leapt on each other, tumbling across the grass.

Claude took his chance and pounced to his feet. 'The magnificent Claude lives to fight another day,' he declared.

Manx gave Claude a tired smile. 'I've had my paws full working on the new fighter planes,' she said. 'Thanks for entertaining these two.'

'Pickle studies every move like a master,' said Claude. 'And Wiggle — well, she has enough energy to take on a whole battalion of guard DOGZ. Soon they'll be teaching *ME* a thing or two,' he added with a laugh. 'But for now, I remain undefeated with my nine lives.'

Wiggle and Pickle suddenly stopped fighting. 'It'th not fair!' Wiggle complained to Manx. 'He was just about to thurrender before *you* came along.'

Picklepurr grinned and moved into Stinging Scorpion position. She pointed to herself. 'What about Claude versus Major Tom,' she challenged.

'Major Tom, timeth two!' cried Wiggle, striking a Crouching Cobra stance beside her sister.

'Looks like Major Tom's going to be your downfall, Claude,' Manx whispered behind her paw. Then she noticed her wristwatch. 'Oh goodness, look at the time! Sorry girls, I have to take your instructor away.' She grabbed Claude. 'Come on. Major Tom's got a *big surprise* for us. The entire squadron will be there.'

# CHAPTER 2

The rat-tat-tat of boots on marble echoed as Claude and Manx hurried up the grand staircase within the chateau's dome. Perched on top of the dome was a turret, which served as HQ's air traffic control. The turret gave spectacular 360-degree views, from the airfield and past the hedge maze all the way around to Paris, with the Eiffel Tower in the distance.

By the time Claude and Manx arrived, the turret was jammed with CATs' top commanders, including Admiral 'Eyepatch' Jellicoe and Queen Vic-Clawria's ambassador, Furgus McLongtail. General Fluffington's tea lady was there too, weaving her way through the crowd serving refreshments. They had all come to view CATs' latest weapon in the war against the DOGZ.

CATs' chief inventor, C-for, moved carefully back and forth, checking cables and turning dials on a large bank of machines.

'Dang and blast it, C-for,' grumbled General Fluffington. 'Will this crazy contraption work?'

C-for flicked a switch and picked up a microphone. There was a low humming noise as the machine warmed up. 'Testing, testing,' he said.

'This is *testing* my patience,' grumbled General Fluffington.

'The circuit's dead — there's something wrong,' frowned C-for. He fidgeted with the dials and spoke into the microphone again. 'This is Ground Control to Major Tom. Can you hear me? Over.'

'Hear you *over* what?' asked General Fluffington.

'You misunderstand, sir,' explained Mr Tiddles, the General's secretary. 'C-for says "over" when he's finished speaking into the radio.'

Suddenly a screech came over the loudspeaker. The noise wobbled and see-sawed, making everyone's fur stand on end. It took a moment to realise that it was just the sound of C-for snoring — the old inventor had fallen asleep at the microphone.

Mr Tiddles gently shook C-for awake. The inventor sat up with a start, without missing a beat. 'This is Ground Control,' he said. 'Over.'

They waited in silence.

Claude's ears pricked up. Something was approaching. Then Claude saw it — a fighter plane aiming straight for the control tower! It was in attack position, coming in low and fast.

The next moment there was a frightening roar. All of CATs' top commanders leapt for cover as the fighter buzzed over the tower, just missing it by metres. Claude raced to the window as the plane dived on the crowd of cats who had gathered on the airstrip. The plane zoomed above their heads. Hats twirled into the air and the windsock flapped frantically in the aircraft's backdraught. Next the plane sped skyward, spiralling in a gigantic arc.

A burst of static crackled out of the loudspeakers, followed by a voice everyone recognised. '*Krrrrkkkk* ... This is Major Tom to Ground Control. Over and out, chums.'

Instantly the crowd erupted into loud cheering and applause.

'It works!' Manx grinned at Claude. 'The first ever ground-to-aircraft radio transmission. With this machine, our pilots will be in contact with each other all the time.'

'Major Tom deserves another medal for this!' cheered General Fluffington.

As soon as Major Tom landed, he was mobbed by
well-wishers and autograph hunters. They hefted
their hero onto their shoulders, while journalists
from the daily newspapers took photos to let their
readers know just what Major Tom was up to.

Claude had also been wondering *just* what Major
Tom was up to. Ever since Claude's adventure in
London, it seemed that he was the only feline on
the planet who felt there was something odd about
CATs' most famous pilot — and it wasn't only that
unbelievable part in Major Tom's autobiography
where he defeated two dogs at once by making them
chase their own tails.

Every now and then, Claude had the strangest feeling that Major Tom was plotting against him. Claude stopped and wondered. He really had to shake some sense into himself ... after all, EVERYONE loved Major Tom. Besides, Claude *had* accidentally destroyed Major Tom's personal plane ... oh ... and then there was that gourmet banquet which had been prepared by Major Tom's mother – Claude didn't want to remember *that* embarrassing evening. Major Tom probably had every reason to be moody towards him, Claude thought to himself. It was probably Claude's own guilt making him imagine the worst.

Claude felt a friendly prod. 'I've got work to do,' said Manx. 'General Fluffington has ordered radios to be installed in the entire CATs squadron.' With that, she headed down to the hangars to work on the brand-new Catproni fighter planes.

# CATPRONI PU55 FIGHTER

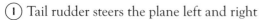

(1) Tail rudder steers the plane left and right

(2) Tail elevators steer the plane up and down

(3) Innovative construction uses a lightweight Duralumin metal framework, instead of the usual wood framework, which can sustain heavy damage from gunfire. Aircraft dope seals the fabric covering, forming a tight skin over the frame

(4) Ailerons on each wing help roll the plane to the left or right

(5) Multiple wing struts, combined with Duralumin frame, give additional strength, and allow the plane to fly at higher speeds and perform sharp turns

(6) Optional rear catpit can be converted into passenger/gunner seat

(7) Pilot's catpit and controls

(8) 2 x Marlin Rockwell M1918 machine guns fire 650 rounds (bullets) per minute. Each gun is 4 kg lighter than the usual Vickers machine gun, and is synchronised with the propeller shaft so bullets don't hit the propeller blade (a design copied from the Fokker triplane)

(9) Engine exhaust

(10) 300 horsepower Catproni V8 engine, produces a top speed of 237 km/hr

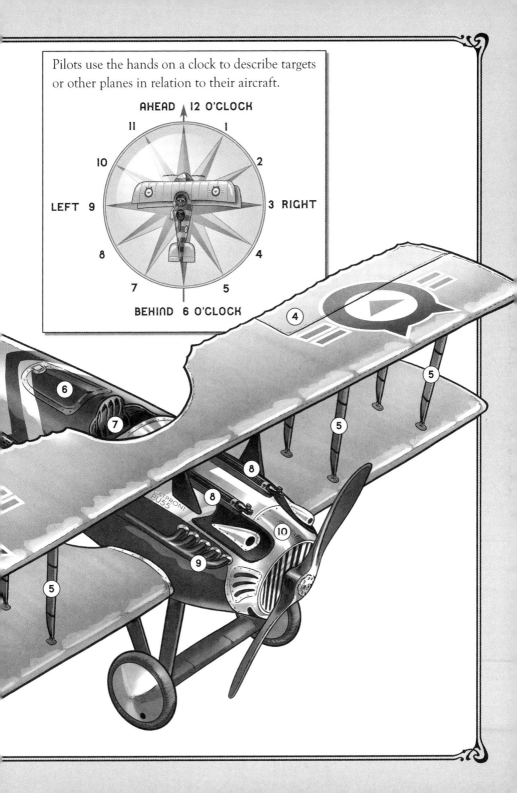

Pilots use the hands on a clock to describe targets or other planes in relation to their aircraft.

AHEAD 12 O'CLOCK

11
1
10
2
LEFT 9 · 3 RIGHT
8
4
7
5

BEHIND 6 O'CLOCK

'It's a beautiful sight,' boomed General Fluffington, as he scanned the planes lined up on the airfield. 'With our ground-to-air radio and our brand-new Catproni fighters, those DOGZ don't have a lick of hope.' He thumped his secretary on the back, and Mr Tiddles almost coughed up a furball. 'Now, Mr Tiddles, is your model completed?' Mr Tiddles nodded. 'Excellent,' murmured General Fluffington. 'Call the pilots to our secret underground command centre for an extra-special tippity-top-secret meeting.'

'With sardines on top?' asked Mr Tiddles.

'Piddling poodles!' bellowed General Fluffington. 'This meeting is so special it's going to be smothered in anchovies and cream! It's time to launch Operation Downfall.'

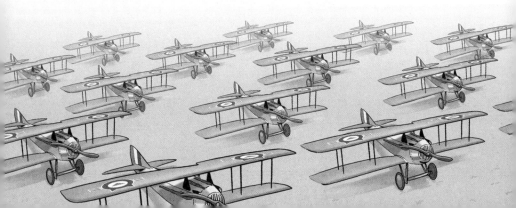

# CHAPTER 3

'Crikey dingo,' grumbled Syd Fishus. 'My uniform must've shrunk at the cleaners.'

Claude's old friend was waiting by the reflection pond in front of CATs HQ. Claude had changed out of his martial arts clothes and was pulling on his jacket, while Syd was fiddling with his buttons as he attempted to squeeze into his own dress uniform. Claude smiled. Together, he and Syd had helped each other out of many close calls, but this was one tight squeeze Syd would have to sort out all by himself.

The two pilots made their way across a bridge to the gazebo sitting in the centre of the reflection pond. Claude checked that no one was looking, then he pulled a lever which revealed the secret entrance to CATs' underground command centre.

# GAZEBO SECRET ENTRANCE
## TO CATs' BASE COMMAND CENTRE

LEVER

Turns off curtain waterfall

Gazebo

Waterfall

Spiral staircase behind waterfall

Base Command Centre

Offices

MAJOR TOM WANTS YOU! TO JOIN THE FIGHT AGAINST EVIL

DESTROY THIS MAD BRUTE ENLIST NOW

Catacombs

The rest of CATs' fighter squadron was already waiting when Claude and Syd arrived at the heavily locked door which led into the command centre. There was an air of excitement swirling around. Everyone was buzzing about the new ground-to-air radio Major Tom had demonstrated – everyone except General Fluffington, that is.

'Blithering bloodhounds!' grumbled the General, patting himself down. 'I seem to have forgotten my blasted keys.' There was a collective groan. This wasn't the first time General Fluffington had locked them out.

At that moment, the door swung open. 'Afternoon,' said General Fluffington's tea lady.

'Mrs Cushion!' thundered General Fluffington. 'What in dog's name are you doing lurking in our secret underground base command?'

'Pouring the tea,' replied Mrs Cushion innocently.

'Oh yes,' said the General, calming himself down. 'As you were, Mrs Cushion, and make mine a double cream ...'

'… with four sugars,' finished Mrs Cushion. She knew all of General Fluffington's little secrets.

As the squadron piled inside, Major Tom pulled General Fluffington aside.

'You should be wary of that tea lady,' warned Major Tom. He was planting the seeds of mischief, so that no one suspected what he was really up to. 'She could be the DOGZ spy we've been looking for all these years.'

'Pish posh,' snorted General Fluffington. 'Mrs Cushion has been my tea lady since I was a kit in nappies. She may be as blind as a naked mole rat, and her tea tastes like aeroplane fuel, but Mrs Cushion is so air-headed that she wouldn't know a single thing that the DOGZ would want.'

From the other side of the room, Claude noticed Mrs Cushion glance his way from behind her bulging milk-bottle glasses. She gave him a sly wink. Claude was one of only three cats who knew that Mrs Cushion was actually the head of CATs Eyes Intelligence

Network. Like the rest of the pilots, she was here for their most important briefing ever.

The small figure of Commander Snookums spoke up. 'We have the DOGZ on the run. Our latest intelligence tells us that they have retreated to the hillside castle of Hundestein.'

'This'll be like catching goldfish in a bowl,' chuckled Syd, puffing on his pipe of catnip.

'That's a revolting habit you have there, Captain Fishus,' frowned Commander Snookums.

'Nothing wrong with catching goldfish in a bowl,' Syd muttered to Claude.

'She's talking about your smoking,' whispered Claude. His old friend had many bad habits, but there was not a single cat whom Claude would rather have watching his back in a dogfight.

'Don't be so cocky, Captain Fishus,' warned Commander Snookums. 'The DOGZ may have backed themselves into a corner, but a cornered dog is a dangerous beast. If this mission is to succeed, it has to be a combined effort. We cannot do it by ourselves. It is time to introduce you to CATs' secret ally.'

A dangerous odour wafted through CATs' command centre. There was a sharp intake of breath as pilots turned and saw a small dog enter the room. Murmurs of shock and surprise swirled through the crowd as the dog strutted boldly to the front of the room and joined Commander Snookums on the stage — as if he belonged there!

'Let me introduce Rex,' said Commander Snookums. 'The leader of The White Paw.'

Claude was thrilled to see the rebel leader. The White Paw were dogs who had turned against the DOGZ army and had been secretly fighting alongside CATs since the war had begun. Claude and Rex had survived two death-defying missions together and many of CATs' victories had only been possible with the help of Rex and his White Paw soldiers. However, not all cats were on such friendly terms with dogs.

Rex spoke with a calm voice. 'I know many of you think that all dogs are bad DOGZ. It may be hard for some of you to believe that I too wish to see the downfall of the DOGZ army. It is of vital importance that we honourable few, we brave cats and dogs, work together to capture Hundestein Castle, and free the treasures within. I will now hand over to General Fluffington to explain our combined plan of attack.'

There was still a lot of muttering about the appearance of a dog in CATs' base command. General Fluffington quietened the pilots with a loud cough.

'The CATs fighter squadron will fly in tight
formation defending a bomber aircraft. The bomber
will blow the gates off Hundestein Castle. While
this is happening, Rex —' the General gave another
sharp cough '— Rex will personally lead a squad of
White Paw commandos, who will storm the castle
as soon as the gates are down. If this surprise attack
goes to plan, we'll have control of the castle before
those mongrels can say Rum Tum Tugger.' General
Fluffington indicated his secretary. 'Mr Tiddles has
constructed a special demonstration.'

Mr Tiddles stepped forward and pulled back
a cloth, revealing a miniature model of
Hundestein Castle, which he had
lovingly constructed in painstakingly
detailed 1/72 scale.

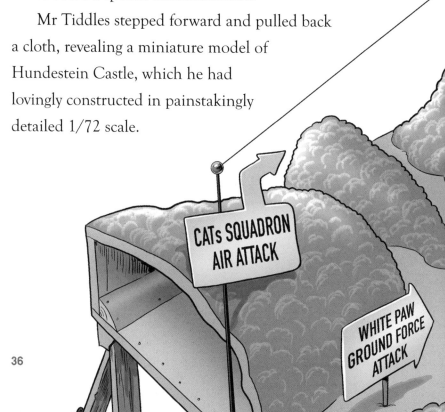

CATs SQUADRON
AIR ATTACK

WHITE PAW
GROUND FORCE
ATTACK

'Why don't we just blow the whole castle to smithereens?' called out Snowy von Fluffytail, one of the pilots.

'Hundestein must *NOT* be destroyed,' spoke up Commander Snookums, with an urgent glance towards Rex. 'There are *vital* treasures within! Before Alf Alpha took over Hundestein, the castle was the grand palace of King Charles Spaniel. Our mission is to bring down the DOGZ, *not* to destroy the treasures of history.'

The pilots began muttering again.

'It's an impenetrable fortress.'

'The DOGZ will shoot us out of the sky.'

'It looks dangerous.'

'Impossible, I say.'

'Balderdash!' boomed General Fluffington, bringing everyone to attention. He may not have liked the idea of fighting alongside rebel dogs, but he was used to following orders. 'Major Tom flew a scouting mission over the castle just this morning.

Isn't that right, Major Tom?'

Major Tom spoke up from the back of the room. 'The castle is *completely* undefended,' he lied.

'Purr-fect,' said General Fluffington, rubbing his paws together. 'This mission will be a total disaster if the DOGZ get their forces into Hundestein. It is essential that we strike immediately. Therefore, Operation Downfall will take place at dawn tomorrow. Mr Tiddles will now demonstrate how this mission will run smoothly.'

Mr Tiddles hung a toy aeroplane on a wire which ran the length of the model he had lovingly constructed in painstakingly detailed 1/72 scale.

GATE

CATs SQUADRON AIR ATTACK

WHITE PAW GROUND FORCE ATTACK

Rex rushed forward and doused the nightmare scene with a bucket of water.

Within moments, Mr Tiddles' model, which he had lovingly constructed in painstakingly detailed 1/72 scale, had been turned into a soggy, smouldering scene of destruction.

Everyone in the room sat in stunned silence.

'Operation Downfall, alright,' muttered Syd.

General Fluffington gave a throaty growl. 'Well, I'm sure the actual mission will be as smooth as puréed jellymeat.' Suddenly his frown turned into a wide grin. 'And we have our first volunteer to lead the mission.' He pointed to the back of the room, where CATs' most famous dogfighter, Major Ginger Tom, had stood up.

When Claude looked back, he got the strangest feeling that Major Tom was actually edging towards the door, rather than volunteering for a dangerous mission.

'Sorry chums,' said Major Tom, as slick as oil. 'Would love to sock it to those dirty DOGZ,' he gave the air a jab with his fist, 'but … ah … you know, my plane was shot up in a dogfight this morning. You know how dangerous it is. I'm sorry to say, but I'm out of action, chums. I'm *devastated* I won't be able to be there with you when it all goes *down* tomorrow.'

Claude leapt to his feet. 'I'll lead the squadron, sir,' he said, without hesitation. When the DOGZ were finally defeated, Claude was determined to be right there, in the heart of the action.

'That's the spirit, my boy!' cheered General Fluffington.

After the pilots had been fully briefed, Claude found a few moments to catch up with The White Paw leader. Rex and Claude chatted about their friends: Buster, Gertie and The White Mouse, until it was time for Rex to leave.

'Sorry, I have to fly,' said Rex. 'Rusty is taking me back to the front lines to prepare our commandos for tomorrow's mission.'

As Rex hurried away, Claude saw a tall, rusty-coloured dog waiting for the rebel leader. Claude smiled, knowing that The Red Setter was now one of The White Paw pilots. Between the rebel commandos and the CATs' new fighter planes, *nothing* would stop CATs from complete victory this time.

ajor Tom slunk out of the meeting. He was in such a hurry that he stopped only twice to check his reflection in windows, making sure that he looked *just* the right mix of dashing and dishevelled. He rushed back to his quarters and locked the door behind him.

Inside, he picked up a pen — but *not* to write his next best-selling autobiography, nor to sign the photographs of himself

which he usually sent to the DOGZ prisoners he had shot down. Instead, Major Tom was going to write a coded message to the DOGZ leader, Alf Alpha.

Major Tom had been promised great rewards for betraying his fellow cats. But so far, Major Tom's

years of spying had earned him
just one little trinket — Alf Alpha
had given Major Tom a bejewelled
kitten on a chain, which was a
one-of-a-kind treasure created by the
famous Russian jeweller Furbergé. It was
encrusted with diamonds and sparkled mysteriously,
as if it had some secret to share. Major Tom reached
into his pocket and pulled out the chain. To his
surprise, the jewelled kitten was no longer attached.

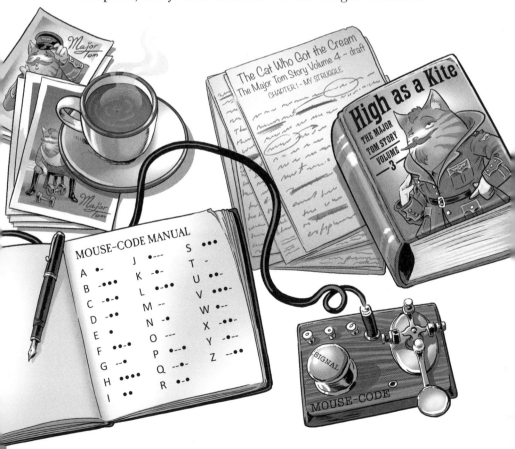

The Cat Who Got the Cream
The Major Tom Story Volume 4 - draft
CHAPTER I - MY STRUGGLE

High as a Kite
THE MAJOR
TOM STORY
VOLUME
— 3 —

MOUSE-CODE MANUAL

A •-       J •---      S •••
B -•••     K -•-      T -
C -•-•     L •-••      U ••-
D -••      M --       V •••-
E •        N -•       W •--
F ••-•     O ---       X -••-
G --•      P •--•      Y -•--
H ••••     Q --•-      Z --••
I ••       R •-•

SIGNAL

MOUSE-CODE

He frantically patted himself down, but he couldn't find the jewelled kitten anywhere.

'Well, tan my hide and call me a tabby!' cursed Major Tom furiously. *Never mind.* He opened a secret compartment in his desk which held a radio transmitter for sending spy messages by mouse-code. After this message had been sent to Alf Alpha, Major Tom would get more than tiny treasures. Once Cat Allied Troops had been defeated, everyone would discover why Major Tom had betrayed them.

Far from CATs HQ, high in his mountaintop lair The Hound's Tooth, Alf Alpha was in a meeting with Edward, the supreme commander of the Woof-Laft (the DOGZ air force). Edward had recently been promoted to Minister of Spying, and he also happened to be … a teddy bear.

General Dogsbody entered and delivered a coded message.

'Look, Edward,' said Alf Alpha gleefully. 'It's from our spy, Tomcat.'

General Dogsbody shook his head. He had
been a loyal soldier for many years, but now it was
clear that Alf Alpha was as deranged as a dog with
rabies. It was no wonder that the DOGZ had been
losing the war. As he backed away slowly, General
Dogsbody wondered if he'd been on the wrong
side all along.

'I've got just the thing for you, young whipper-
snapper,' said C-for. Claude and Syd had come to
visit CATs' crazy inventor before Operation Downfall.

'You need all the help you can get to beat the
DOGZ army, and I've been working on this little
puppy for years,' said C-for proudly.

'Let me guess,' said Syd. 'You came
up with it in a dream?'

'How did you know?' replied
C-for seriously. 'Dreams are
realms of magic, my boy. In fact,
I've been studying the greatest
dreamer of all time — Lionardo
da Vinci. He dreamed up the
most incredible inventions.
Lionardo's ideas were centuries
ahead of their time.'

THE GENIUS OF
LIONARDO

TROJAN DOG BONE

CAT-A-PULT

'So, where is this latest invention you've dreamed up?' asked Claude.

'I'm sitting on it,' said C-for. 'I call it the "Dream Seat". It's a massage chair, to relax you.'

'Looks like it would relax you to sleep,' whispered Syd.

'That's not a good idea for a pilot,' Claude murmured back.

'Exactly what I thought!' beamed C-for. 'It *IS* a good idea for a pilot, isn't it? After all, a comfortable pilot is a focused pilot. That's why I've installed a prototype version in your plane.'

C-for flicked a switch on his Dream Seat and leaned back.

'*Ahhhh,*' sighed the old inventor, closing his eyes. 'But I must warn you …'

'Warn us what?' asked Claude. But C-for had fallen fast asleep in the softly vibrating chair. Claude turned to Syd. 'Let's go and make sure C-for's dozy invention hasn't damaged my brand-new fighter plane.'

'This aircraft is a total disaster,' said Manx.

Claude and Syd were standing in the hangar, where CATs' head engineer was working on a damaged fighter plane.

'I just don't understand,' said Manx, sliding out from under the fuselage. 'This plane is brand-new. And this damage … well, it's very strange. It's going to take me days to fix, plus I've got to install radio transmitters into all the planes before tomorrow's big mission.' With a sigh, she climbed up into the catpit and began working away under the canopy.

'Yes, C-for warned us about the planes,' said Claude.

Manx popped her head out of the catpit. 'What kind of warning?'

'I'll tell you what kind of warning,' snorted Syd. 'A warning that C-for's inventions never work the way they're supposed to.'

'Oh, you're talking about C-for's "Dream Seat",' laughed Manx, getting back to her work. 'I've double-checked *your* plane, Claude, and there's nothing you need to be worried about. *This* plane, on the other paw ...'

Claude was lost in thought. He was remembering his last adventure to Russia, when he'd received another kind of warning. An old gypsy woman had given Claude a tiny jewelled kitten encrusted with diamonds. The gypsy had foretold that this trinket would reveal Claude's true enemy — but soon after, the jewelled kitten had been stolen by DOGZ soldiers.

Claude felt Syd nudge him.

'Mate, are you listening?' asked Syd, twitching a quizzical ear.

'Sorry,' said Claude. 'I was just thinking that we still have a DOGZ spy lurking amongst us.' He decided not to say anything about the Russian gypsy and the jewelled kitten. In truth, Claude thought it was a crazy fantasy that a diamond-encrusted trinket could reveal his true enemy.

'Yeah — if only we had some way to identify the back-stabbing traitor,' growled Syd.

'It's that dratted Major Tom,' said Manx from within the catpit.

'Major Tom?' said Claude, suddenly alert. 'Major Tom is the traitor?'

'What? No,' laughed Manx. She stopped what she was doing and sat up on the edge of the catpit. 'I was just complaining to myself. See, this is Major Tom's plane. He's to blame for all this extra work. I don't understand how some of these bullet holes got here. It's like someone took out a pistol and shot up the wings. And the fuel pipes and aileron cables look as if they were slashed on purpose! Major Tom must have been in one *unbelievable* dogfight to get this kind of damage.'

'You've obviously got your paws full,' said Claude. 'And we need a good night's catnap. Come on Syd, we've got the mission of our lives tomorrow.'

As Claude and Syd walked off, Manx noticed something catch the light in the bottom of Major Tom's catpit. She leaned down and fidgeted about, until her claws clutched something. When she brought it into the light, she caught her breath. In her paw was a miniature jewelled kitten which sparkled and shimmered as if it were alive.

'This must have fallen out of Major Tom's pocket while he was flying,' Manx said to herself. 'Claude! Syd! Look at this!' she called out — but the two pilots had gone. 'Shame, I'm sure Claude would have been interested to see this. I had better make sure it gets back to Major Tom.' Manx popped the jewelled kitten in her pocket.

Claude had no idea just how right he'd been. Tomorrow really *was* going be the fight of their lives.

# CHAPTER 5

**B**efore dawn the next morning, the entire CATs squadron was assembled on the airstrip. A huge crowd from the medical wing, as well as ground crew and staff from HQ, had come to send off the pilots. General Fluffington paced back and forth, giving the squadron its final instructions. Behind them, the new Catproni fighter planes sat gleaming as the sun started to creep over the horizon. A roaring chorus echoed across the airfield as the ground crew fired up the engines in the cold morning air.

Major Tom stood nearby, with a simpering smile stretched across his face.

As General Fluffington ordered the pilots to their planes, he turned to Major Tom and placed a heavy paw on the Major's shoulder. 'I know how desperately you wanted to be part of this. It doesn't seem right that our greatest hero should miss out on the dogfight to end all dogfights.'

'It's a dratted shame,' sighed Major Tom dramatically. Inside, he was grinning as he imagined the final destruction of the entire CATs Air Corps and the troublesome White Paw rebels.

'Well, no more wallowing in your worries!' boomed General Fluffington. 'I've got a *wonderful* surprise for you!'

Mr Tiddles hurried over carrying a fur-lined flying jacket and goggles. 'I know your own aircraft is damaged,' said the General, 'so I've arranged for you to be a spotter and radio operator in our lead plane.'

Major Tom stood there, dumbfounded. For once he had no smart comeback nor easy laugh.

'I can see you're speechless,' continued the General. 'Claude's going to be thrilled to have an extra pair of eyes watching his back for enemies.'

Just then Claude rushed over. 'Come on, Tom!' he cheered. 'It's time to kick the tyres and light the fires. We're the lead fighter — everyone's waiting.'

Major Tom gave an awkward gulp. He quickly glanced around for a way out — but the crowd had come to cheer on their greatest hero. They lifted Major Tom onto their shoulders and helped him into the rear catpit of Claude's plane.

'It … it … it wasn't supposed to be like this,' stammered a bewildered Major Tom.

Claude clambered into the pilot's seat. 'Exciting, isn't it!' he shouted over the roaring engines. Amongst the noisy onlookers, Claude spotted Manx, waving to him from the back of the crowd. Something glinted in her paw, and it seemed as if she had important news to tell him. But Operation Downfall could wait no longer. 'Let's go,' said Claude. 'Today's going to be a blast.'

Claude and Major Tom weaved though the mountains towards Hundestein Castle. The massive squadron of CATs fighters had to stay low if there was any chance of taking the DOGZ by surprise.

As lead aircraft, Claude's job was to scout ahead. In the rear catpit, Major Tom was looking out for enemy fighters and gun positions, and reporting on the new radio system. The rest of the squadron followed a few moments behind, defending the gigantic bomber which would blow the castle gates off. Once that was done, The White Paw would storm the castle and Operation Downfall would be complete.

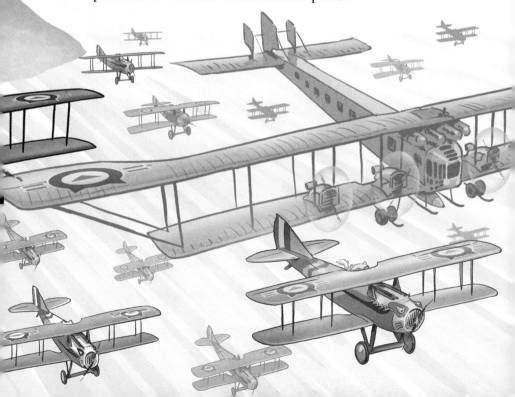

Claude's brand-new plane was incredible. It could gain height in a flash, and dive as smoothly as a falcon. Usually, even in the best fighter planes, it was a battle to wrestle the controls against the powerful spinning engine. But the joystick in the Catproni PU55 was as light as a feather, responding to Claude's slightest touch.

The peaceful morning air was shattered by the roar of engines as Claude and Major Tom entered a narrow valley cloaked with dark forested hills. At the head of the valley, Claude spied Hundestein Castle — the DOGZ' last stronghold. 'Target in sight,' he confirmed over the radio. 'All clear for our final attack.' An ominous drone followed, as the rest of the squadron swept into the valley.

As they sped towards the castle, Major Tom sat fretting and fussing in the rear catpit. They were entering a trap that he had planned for months, and he was in a terrible dilemma.

All these years Major Tom had vowed
to fight for DOGZ' success. But there was
something else he cared about far more
than the DOGZ … himself!

'This is crazy,' Major Tom said over
the radio.

'That's the spirit,' replied Claude.
'We're almost there.'

'No, really …' stammered Major Tom.
They sped closer and closer to the trap.
'It's … it's …'

'What is it?' yelled Claude.

'To your left!' cried Major Tom.
'Guns, at 10 o'clock!'

Claude saw a bright explosion of light from within the forested hills. In the next second, the sound wave hit them — it was the boom of a Howlitzer cannon and a flaming roar as a shell whizzed past. It exploded in a fury of flying shrapnel just metres away from them.

'Anti-aircraft guns!' Claude yelled into his radio. He had just enough time to warn the rest of the squadron. 'It's an ambush!'

With that, the hillside burst into a wall of flashes. Balls of smoke erupted all around.

Claude dipped his wing and it snagged on a treetop. For a moment, the plane began a dangerous spin — but miraculously they were flung away from the spot where an anti-aircraft shell would have directly hit their aircraft. Claude had to use all his skill to keep the plane from spiralling into the forest.

Claude pulled them level and was faced with a terrible realisation — he couldn't escape! This trap had been well set. If he flew up, he'd be an easy target silhouetted against the sky. His only choice was to try and outfly the gunners. By keeping low and speeding fast against the treetops, he'd be a much harder target to track. He powered the Catproni up to full speed.

Now the DOGZ let loose with all their firepower. Machine-gun bullets cut through the explosions, with tracer fire lighting up the smoke like hundreds of tiny comets. But the DOGZ had never seen anything as fast as this new plane. Their shots flew wildly off-target.

Everything was happening in a blur. Smoke and explosions filled the air. It seemed as if every space was filled with a burst of anti-aircraft fire and pieces of metal shell slicing through the smoke. There was no doubt that the DOGZ had been tipped off. But there was no time for Claude to think about traitors now. This time he was *really* flying to save his nine lives.

Claude was stunned at Major Tom's impossible skill as a spotter. The Major had an almost *magical* ability to spot the DOGZ' hidden guns. He seemed to know their firing patterns and just how to avoid them! Claude ducked and dived as he followed Major Tom's directions. They skimmed the treetops so close they were in danger of losing their landing gear — until suddenly they were clear. They had burst free from the smoke and shellfire.

Claude glanced back. The peaceful valley had become a wall of gunfire, completely impossible for the rest of the squadron to fly through. The other planes had broken off the attack and were turning away from the guns. But then Claude's heart jumped as he saw another ambush swooping down the mountains — DOGZ' fighter planes had begun to attack the CATs' squadron from behind!

Over the radio they heard HQ issuing instructions. 'Call off the attack. Retreat to base.'

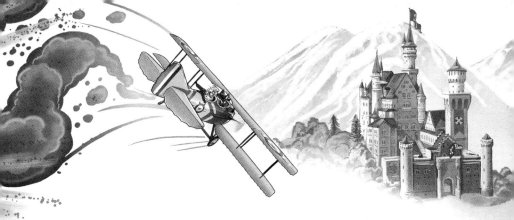

Somehow, Claude and Major Tom had made it through. They were all alone, with nothing between them and the castle. Claude straightened up and sped directly towards Hundestein.

'What are you doing?' howled Major Tom. 'Didn't you hear the order? Retreat! The plan is kaput!'

'I've never been one for following orders,' yelled Claude. 'Not while we can save the mission. If we shoot out those gates, The White Paw can still take the castle.' He cocked the Catproni's two Marlin Rockwell M1918 machine guns, and eased his finger on the trigger.

DOGZ' soldiers hadn't expected a fighter plane to get this far. They rushed to the castle walls and began taking pot shots at the lone attacking aircraft. This was a game of nerves. Claude gritted his teeth and flew directly at them.

Major Tom was cowering in his catpit when a direct shot hit the engine. The motor erupted in a cloud of smoke and the plane lurched sickeningly downwards.

'Stop shooting!' cried Major Tom over the noise. 'It's ME! Major Tom!'

'You may be famous at home, but I'm sure they don't care about you here,' yelled Claude. He'd tried his best, but now he'd lost all control of the plane. He braced himself as they plummeted towards the castle walls.

CHAPTER 6

Claude and Major Tom were headed for total destruction as the plane went down in a flurry of smoke.

In his panic, Major Tom's paw brushed a switch. At once C-for's massage chairs began to vibrate. While it was indeed the perfect time for a soothing massage to ease an incredibly stressful situation, C-for's inventions rarely worked as intended.

The massage chairs gave a violent jolt. The mechanics connected to the engine had been shot to pieces, and the pressure on the internal springs was simply too much. Without warning, the chairs sprang into the air, taking the pilots with them …

Claude landed with a tearing, snapping crash.

For a moment he was dazed, but when he cleared his head Claude found that nothing was broken, except a few branches … he had been caught by a tree. He looked down to see that Major Tom had also been caught — except Major Tom had been caught by DOGZ soldiers!

A squad of DOGZ was lurking around another tree, where the Catproni PU55 had crashed. *I'll have to slip away while the DOGZ are barking up the wrong tree*, Claude thought to himself. He shimmied down to the cobbled courtyard and peeked around the wide trunk. Major Tom was surrounded by a troop of Sniffer DOGZ, talking with a defiant expression on his face. Claude could only imagine what courageous words his fellow pilot was telling them.

Major Tom saw Claude across the courtyard. The DOGZ followed Major Tom's gaze and turned in Claude's direction. 'There he is! Nab him!' yelled one of the DOGZ.

Claude dashed for cover. He sped around a corner and found stairs leading off in all directions.

He had no idea which way to go. The stomp of DOGZ boots was getting closer. Then he noticed a pile of boxes. He quickly hid inside one, and peeked out through its hand-hold.

Two soldiers belted around the corner. These Sniffer DOGZ had a ferocious sense of smell. One was a rough Alsatian, with a wolf-like face. He took a deep breath through his nose and swivelled his big head back and forth, then approached Claude's hiding place suspiciously. Claude held his breath in fear. He was certain he would be sniffed out this time.

SNIFF
SNIFF
SNIFF

SNIFF
SNIFF

'Ease up, Bruno!' called another dog. 'Don't get in a slather over jellymeat again. Come on, the cat must've gone this way.' With that, the two DOGZ raced off.

Claude breathed a sigh of relief. Luckily the smell of DOGZ rations had disguised his scent.

Claude doubled back the way he had come. He followed unseen as the soldiers took Major Tom into the castle. It appeared they were taking the Major down into the dungeon. Other DOGZ were moving in and out of the dungeon too, carrying huge paintings and boxes of treasure. Claude knew that the DOGZ used all sorts of torture on their prisoners. He was torn. On one paw he was desperate to stage a rescue before the DOGZ could tickle Major Tom's tummy or tug on his tail. But on the other paw, Claude had a much more important mission to complete.

If the DOGZ got their defences into the castle, it would be impossible to get them out, and the battles would continue for years and years. He *had* to get the gates open before it was too late.

Moving as quietly as a cat at midnight, Claude climbed up the castle walls. He looked down into the main courtyard and was shocked by what he saw.

The castle was far from undefended!

A small squad of DOGZ troops was lined up, as well as motorbikes, armoured tanks and large cannons. Behind the troops, Claude could see the main gates — he had to find some way to get past those troops and open them.

Then Claude saw just what he needed. It was up to him to save this mission and he was going to have to do something as *unbelievable* as any of the stories in Major Tom's autobiography.

Nearby was a wooden catapult, just like the ones designed by Lionardo da Vinci that Claude had seen in C-for's workshop. The catapult was an ancient defence which hadn't been used for centuries – but it might just do the trick.

If Claude could heave the catapult into the right position, he'd be able to send himself soaring above the heads of the DOGZ soldiers, open the gate and save the day.

Just then a familiar voice startled him.

Claude spun around to
see his old comrade, Major Tom,
striding towards him like the cat who ate the canary.

'How did you get away?' frowned Claude.

'It's time you realised that it's over,' smiled
Major Tom. 'The war's finished. *We* won.'

There was something very odd about the way
Major Tom was smirking. Claude was wondering
what on earth Tom was talking about when a great
commotion erupted from *within* the castle.

There were yelps and barks and a thunderous stomp of boots, but it wasn't DOGZ soldiers — it was The White Paw! Within moments the courtyard was swarming with rebels. The small squad of DOGZ was so outnumbered that it surrendered without a fight.

'I can't believe it!' cried Claude. Somehow Rex and his army had broken into the castle through a secret entrance. Major Tom was utterly stunned when Claude leapt up and hugged him. 'You were right! It's all over,' Claude cheered. 'We won!'

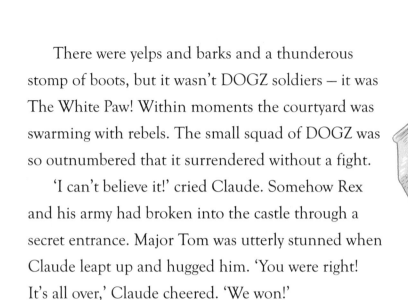

# CHAPTER 7

Rex and his army swept through the castle, rounding up the last of the DOGZ soldiers. The rebel leader knew every corner and hiding place and The White Paw hung their banners from the highest towers. It was a moment of sweet victory after years of war.

The White Paw soldiers raised their leader onto their shoulders. Claude and Major Tom followed behind as Rex was paraded through the castle's grand hall. Rex was obviously loved by his troops, and they placed him on a raised platform at the far end of the hall, in front of an old throne. The great golden chair had not been sat on since Alf Alpha and his DOGZ army had brought war to the once peaceful kingdoms of Europe.

Behind the throne was a gigantic red banner of Alf Alpha, stretching from the floor to the ceiling. Rex's second-in-command, Buster, called on their most powerful soldier to tear it down.

The Mighty Osman, a great Alaskan malamute, lumbered onto the stage. He yanked downwards and the banner tore loose. There was an awed silence as the red fabric tumbled to the floor. Claude gasped when he saw the huge mural revealed underneath.

MAGNUS REX CANIS

The assembled troops all bowed before Rex.

'Long live, King Charles Spaniel,' Buster called out. He read the latin motto on the mural. 'Rex Magnus Canis — the Great Dog King.'

The crowd howled and cheered in approval. Claude smiled to himself — he had suspected that Rex was more than your average canine. No wonder Rex had known the secret entrances to the castle. Hundestein was *his* royal palace.

At that moment there was a yelping commotion from the back of the hall. A pair of dogs rushed past Claude and leapt onto King Charles. Buster and the other top commanders stood aside and simply watched as the dogs pinned the king to the floor. They were followed by an elegant spaniel with long flowing ears who rushed forward, crying 'Pups, pups, get off your father!'

King Charles laughed as he scrambled to his feet and embraced his whole family. This was Rex's true treasure. His family had been impounded in the dungeons since the start of the war. The royal dog family were finally reunited.

# the Scratching

# DOGZ LICKED!

**Our intrepid war reporter, Fifi Hackles, can now reveal news of a secret operation.** Yesterday, an attack on the DOGZ stronghold of Hundestein was a decisive victory for CATs. Commander Snookums at CATs HQ announced that 'Operation Downfall' went exactly as planned, with King Charles Spaniel leading his troops in a surprise attack through secret tunnels. England's Queen Vic-Clawria sent warm greetings, welcoming back the true dog king, heralding a reign of peace and friendship between cats and dogs. During party celebrations today, Queen Vic-Clawria's ambassador Furgus McLongtail almost started a new war when he played his bagpipes. READ ALL THE DETAILS ON PAGE 3

KING CHARLES SPANIEL, REUNITED WITH HIS FAMILY, QUEEN SHEBA, PRINCE CHARLES AND PRINCESS SISI

# Post

EDITOR IN CHIEF D. MURRAY. PUBLISHED BY CHAPMAN & CO. SINCE 1822

# DOG GONE

THE HOUND'S TOOTH, ABANDONED

Alf Alpha has fled his mountaintop hideout, The Hound's Tooth. CATs Eyes Intelligence Network want to discover his new secret lair and stop this trouble-making sausage dog from stirring up more mischief and mayhem.

## RED SETTER — EVERY DOG HAS HIS DAY

The Red Setter had his moment of redemption when he came to the rescue of CATs' fighter planes. Affectionately named 'Rusty' by The White Paw, he helped defeat the DOGZ air force in yesterday's attack.
He was tipped off by Alf Alpha's second-in-command, General Dogsbody, who suspected The Furrer had rabies.
Wing Commander Giggles, of the DOGZ Woof-Laft, was captured after the battle.
'It's not my fault, I'm not a bad dog,' he giggled.
'But when I see a cat I just have to chase it.'

WING COMMANDER GIGGLES BECAME THE DOGZ' TOP FIGTHER PILOT AFTER THE RED SETTER DEFECTED TO THE WHITE PAW

'Crikey dingo mate, you should've seen the battle. This old dog wasn't so "Rusty" after all.' Syd was standing with his arm around Baron von Wolfred, the dog formerly known as The Red Setter, telling Claude about their great victory. The friends were gathered in the grand hall at Hundestein Castle. The battle was won and the war was all but over. It was time to celebrate.

'I was tipped off about the DOGZ ambush by one of Alf Alpha's generals,' said The Red Setter. 'Luckily I knew all the moves of the DOGZ pilots — after all, I trained them! I can't believe I used to be one of those mongrels.' He waved to someone in the crowd and excused himself, leaving the two cats to talk alone.

BARON COSMO!

'Operation Downfall would have been a dog's breakfast if Baron von Wolfred hadn't joined us,' said Syd. 'His squadron of White Paw pilots got us out of that dirty DOGZ ambush.'

Claude screwed up his face. 'We still haven't discovered who it was who betrayed our plans to the DOGZ all those years.'

'Crikey, speaking of discovered,' said Syd, fumbling in his jacket. 'I was supposed to give you this.'

Claude's eyes nearly popped out of their sockets when he saw what was in Syd's paw. It was the tiny jewelled kitten that had been stolen from him by the DOGZ. Only someone who was secretly on the DOGZ side could have got their paws on it.

'Wh ... where did you get this?' he stammered.

'Pretty fancy, isn't it?' said Syd casually. 'Manx gave it to me back at HQ.'

*Manx?!*

Claude's head was reeling. His dear friend couldn't possibly be the DOGZ spy … could she?

'She asked me to give it to you,' Syd continued. 'Manx wanted you to pass it on to its owner – she discovered it in Major Tom's plane.'

'Major Tom!' exclaimed Claude. *Of course!* So Major Tom had been the spy all along. Claude *should* have trusted his cat instincts, but he'd been blinded by Major Tom's fame – they *all* had! Who would ever have been suspicious of the most famous dogfighter in all of katdom?

There was no time to waste with explanations and plans. Claude had to act immediately, before it was too late. He snatched the kitten from Syd and raced off, leaving his friend with a bewildered expression on his face.

Claude hurried through the crowd. He'd seen Major Tom earlier, heading down to the castle dungeon. As Claude clattered down the stairs he was certain that the traitorous orange oaf was up to no good.

Hundestein dungeon was a vaulted cavern beneath the castle. Inside the dungeon were murky cells, where Rex's family had been kept all those years. There were vast, haphazard piles of art and treasure everywhere, which the DOGZ had stolen from all over Europe and hoarded in Hundestein. Claude was thinking that these treasures could now be returned to their rightful owners when he noticed something terrifying.

Slotted amongst the priceless pieces were sticks of dynamite with fuses snaking wildly throughout the dungeon. The whole place was rigged to explode! Just then, Claude felt an explosion of pain on the back of his head. He collapsed in a heap on the stone floor, and his world became cold darkness.

# CHAPTER

Claude opened his eyes groggily. He had only been unconscious for a few moments. As his head cleared, he discovered Major Ginger Tom standing above him with a pistol. Claude realised that he must have been walloped on the head with the pistol grip.

'So you're the purr-petrator!' said Claude, rubbing his aching head.

'Feeling a bit sour, puss?' laughed Major Tom. 'You just can't keep from sniffing around in my doings, can you?'

'It's hard not to, when your *doings* stink so much,' replied Claude. 'I know you're Alf Alpha's vile pet.'

'Yes,' gloated Major Tom. 'Did it never occur to you why the DOGZ didn't have me chained up when you came to "rescue" me all those years ago on your first mission? You fool!' he scoffed. 'Remember when we escaped from Schloss Slobberchop? … *I* shot the tail out of our plane on purpose, hoping to land us in DOGZ territory. On your next mission *I* tried to shoot you and Syd down when you were flying that DOGZ fighter plane. *I* organised the great ambush over Holland, and *I* was the DOGZ "*major* tip-off" on your mission to Egypt. My greatest disappointment was that I couldn't stop you bringing Valentino Catproni to London — that, and your miraculous rescue of The White Paw in Russia after I'd betrayed them to the DOGZ! You always managed to outdo me at the last minute. How did you do it this time?'

Claude pulled out the jewelled kitten.

'Yes, Alf Alpha does like shiny treasures,' purred Major Tom, and he waved his pistol at the piles of stolen artworks. 'But if he can't have them, then no one will.' Major Tom revealed an explosive device rigged with a timer. 'We wired the entire castle with explosives,' he grinned. 'Every enemy of Alf Alpha is above us. When this timer goes off, it will blow you miserable moggies and those White Paw pooches back to the Bone Age.'

'But why?' said Claude. 'Why betray your fellow felines? You're a cat, just like the rest of us.'

'I'm *nothing* like the rest of you *common* furballs!' screamed Major Tom. 'My nanny promised me that I would have everything I wanted when I grew up. I'm descended from Queen Ginger the First of England. I want to be king. I DESERVE to be king! Alf Alpha promised me these things and more … no one will ever call me Gingey Whinge or Tomcat once I'm king of all cats.'

Claude gave a bored groan. 'The only reason I'm listening to your supercilious speech is because you knocked me senseless. If I wasn't as weak as a kitten, I'd crawl out of earshot. You're just a slave to a mad dog — a cowardly puppet.'

'I'm not a coward!' yelled Major Tom. Flecks of spit flew out of his mouth. 'Can a puppet do this?'

With that, he turned the timer on his bomb and set it ticking.

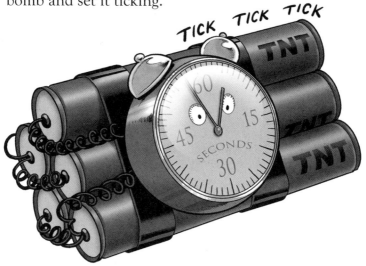

'You came here to celebrate the downfall of the DOGZ army, but very soon it will be Alf Alpha who is celebrating *your* downfall.' Major Tom waved his pistol airily. 'Sorry CHUM, but I have to skedaddle. I have a plane waiting beside the castle. Soon I'll be winging my way to Alf Alpha's secret lair, but you'll be hiss-tory.' He gave a smug look. 'I'd better start preparing for my wedding … once Alf Alpha has made me King Ginger the First, I'll make Princess Kitty my bride.'

'Now I've heard it all,' said Claude. 'I've always been curious why anyone would betray their own side.'

'You should have known,' sneered Major Tom, 'that curiosity killed the cat.' He cocked his pistol and aimed it at Claude. 'I'd say it's been nice knowing you, but actually you've been an annoying prickle in my paw.' He gave an evil chuckle. 'You said today would be a blast—'

At that moment Claude kicked out with his foot, sending Major Tom's pistol flying. Claude sprang to his paws, adopting the Meow-zaki stance known as Stinging Scorpion. He was expertly trained, but his latest trick had been learnt from Wigglebum and Picklepurr — he'd just been 'playing dead' so he could find out every detail of Major Tom's plan.

'You're not getting away this time!' cried Claude.

Claude moved with lightning speed.
He managed to catch katdom's most famous statue
before it was shattered to smithereens.

Major Tom took his chance to flee up the stairs.
Before he escaped, he turned back with an evil grin.
'You can either chase me … or try to stop the bomb,
and save your friends.'

Claude carefully eased the priceless artwork onto the stone floor. His eyes darted up the stairs where Major Tom had fled. This was no time to hesitate. He snatched up the bomb and hurried to the dungeon windows. He tried to shove it between the bars, but it was impossible.

*Tick, tick, tick.*

Claude looked at the timer with horror. The bomb would go off in less than a minute! He had no time to spare.

If the timer went off anywhere near Hundestein, it would set off a chain of explosives rigged throughout the entire castle.

Claude had to get the bomb far away. He dashed up the stairs. As soon as he was outside, he looked around desperately.

From the great hall, Claude could hear the celebrations still going on. They were completely unaware of the terrible threat that was about to destroy them all. Claude hurried to the top of the battlements and looked out over the main courtyard. Snippets of traditional dog songs wafted merrily through the castle.

*Tick, tick, tick.*

Below, the DOGZ prisoners were held under guard. He couldn't throw the bomb down there!

*Tick, tick, tick.*

He turned and peered over the castle's outer walls. He was about to let the bomb fall from his paws, when he saw a mother squirrel and her babies nesting in the trees far below. He couldn't drop it on them!

*Tick, tick, tick.*

*Think, Claude, THINK!*

Then Claude saw something that gave him an idea.

Claude sprinted to the end of the wall. There, facing out over the valley, was the old catapult. Claude dumped the bomb in the catapult's bucket and prayed it was still working.

*Tick, tick, tick.*

He flashed his claws, slashing the ropes which held back the catapult's throwing arm. It flung the bomb in a great arc, far out from the clifftop castle.

SLASH

PING

# KABOOM!

**Claude staggered unsteadily, his ears ringing from the explosion.**

A crowd began to pour out of the grand hall to see what had happened. White Paw guards were running up to the battlements.

'What the blazes is going on?!' bellowed General Fluffington. He looked up at Claude. 'Can you hear me up there?'

But through the ringing and the commotion, Claude heard another sound — an aircraft engine revving for take-off.

If Claude was going to wrap up this mission he was going to have to do something totally heroic and crazy — the type of thing Major Tom had never, *ever*, done, despite what it said in his autobiographies. Claude snatched up one of the huge White Paw banners and hurled himself over the wall.

Major Tom glanced back and saw Claude clawing his way up the fuselage. The Major gave a crazed bark of laughter. 'You just don't know when to quit!' he howled. He flung the plane left, and then right, but when he looked back Claude was still there.

Hundestein Valley was soon left behind, and they soared high above the snowy alps. Claude clung on for dear life as the jagged slopes and icy ravines passed underneath.

'You may have stopped my bomb from destroying your allies,' Major Tom yelled over his shoulder, 'but you're the only one who knows that I was the spy. Didn't your mother ever tell you – you'd better not mess with Major Tom? As long as me and Alf Alpha are still out there, our dream of a pure-bred world will live on – but you won't! It's high time your nine lives ran out for good … *old chum*!'

Claude had heard more than enough from Major Tom for one day. Suddenly, he had one of his most brilliant ideas. It was incredibly risky, but he was quickly running out of time to wrap up this adventure.

Claude had only ever read about the Meow-zaki move called Flying Phoenix. He had never seen someone even attempt the dangerous stunt, but he was going to try it right now!

Claude closed his eyes.

He sucked in a deep breath of air.

But suddenly, Major Tom twirled the plane in a violent corkscrew …